ZODIACTS
Scorpio Skullduggery

I0550642

Written and Illustrated by

Donna McGarry

ZODIACTS
Scorpio Skullduggery

© 2016 by Donna McGarry
© All rights reserved
ISBN 978-0-9982201-0-9

@ariesadventure
Visit us @ zodiacts.com
Printed in the U.S.A.
Published in Nyack, N.Y. by Pollux Ink
Division of Zodiacts

ZODIACTS
Scorpio Skullduggery

Thanks to my newfound (many times removed) cousin Anne Mallahan Mikolay, who reminded me riches come in all kinds of packages. I also wish to thank all the intense, passionate Scorpios I have had the pleasure and fear of knowing. As always, deep gratitude to my brother Michael and my niece Samantha.

Love to all,
Donna

SCORPIO MOON

The Scorpio Moon is intense and dramatic.
Infused with passion, it can be quite traumatic.
Nerves on edge, a little wary,
Ordinary things can seem quite scary.

Piercing stares, a sense of danger,
Penetrating minds, friend or stranger?
Ominous, stubborn, dark and brooding,
Compulsive thoughts prove most intruding.

Sinister, shadowy, murky and suspicious,
Motives are suspect, intentions duplicitous.
Forceful, intuitive, compelling, prophetic,
Irresistable, powerful, alluring, magnetic.

Under the cloud of the
SCORPIO MOON

Kitty, usually flamboyant, proud and intrusive
Becomes fixated, obsessive, and quite reclusive.

Leo, friendly, warm and enjoys being cozy
Dons his Sherlock and gets downright nosy.

Mommy, normally philantropically zealous
Turns possessive, anxious and insanely jealous.

Grannitaurus, a down-to-earth, hard-working mama
Surrounds herself with intrigue and drama.

Daddy, stern, private, business-like and royal
Becomes fiercely devoted, cryptic and loyal.

In the middle of the night, Leo wakes up with a scream...

'Granny is dead,' he cries!
'Relax Leo,' consoles Mom, 'it was just a bad dream.'

'Have some breakfast,' pleads Mom. 'What's your hurry?'

Business to tend to,' quips Dad. 'It's nothing. Don't worry.'

'I'm concerned about your father. He's been acting so strange.'

'Skulking about at all hours, he seems quite deranged.'

'What is going on in that workroom? I have to find out!'

Can you see what all the cloak and dagger behavior is about?'

'Looks like he's obsessed with a photo or blueprint.'

'Try a peek at his zodiac chart. That could provide a hint.'

'An 8th house progression; finally a breakthrough!'

'I still can't piece it together. I'm desperate for a clue.'

'Well, the 8th house refers to purging, psychic powers and rebirth
As well as legacies, inheritances, and other people's worth.'

'That's it, KIT!'

'I'm loathe to spy, Leo, but I'm sounding the alarm…

I'm tailing your father to Grannitaurus' farm.'

'Oh dear, Granny appears to be under the weather.'

'In times of crisis, shouldn't we all band together!'

'Will you please tell me why you are being so mysterious?'

'I'm afraid Granny's condition has grown downright serious.'

'She's confused and babbling about her family bequest.'

'Buried out here somewhere is a secret treasure chest.'

'I'm remembering a tune from the past. How did it go?'

"40 paces from the apple tree
Jump back 10, face east, you will see,
Rows and rows, and rows and a rose,
The answer to your money woes."

'Look, there it is, I knew it all along!'
'Just like Gran sang it in the song.'

What could it be, dad? Diamonds, platinum, fossilized slugs?
Legos, baseball cards, amber insect bugs!'

'What riches are in there, Granny? Gold? Silver? Bonds? Stocks?

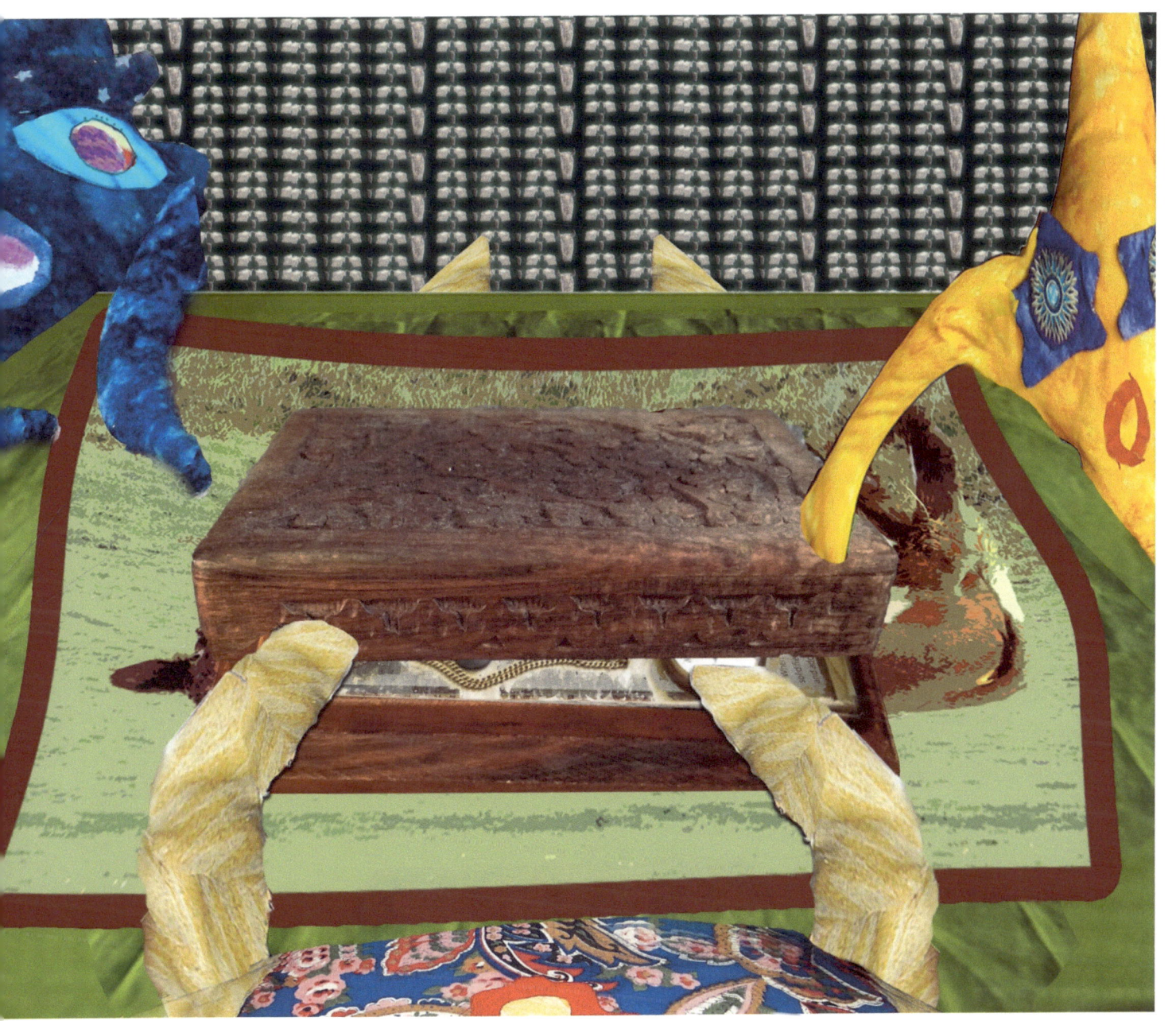

'Way more valuable…

'The Taurus Family Recipe Box'.

'Gran, you've been revived. You're brimming with health!'

'Proving the point, "One man's junk is another man's wealth."'

'What a disappointment. This was no thriller!
I knew from the get-go, the kitty was the killer.'

'Well, we didn't find a chest full of silver or money,
But you looked mighty cute in that Mata Hari getup, honey.'

www.ingramcontent.com/pod-product-compliance
Lightning Source LLC
Chambersburg PA
CBHW041557120626
46551CB00002B/237